Originally published in France by Éditions du Seuil in 2003 under the title *Hôtel d'été.*

Copyright © 2003 by Éditions du Seuil.
Original ISBN 2-02-053040-6.
English translation copyright © 2004 by Éditions du Seuil.

Cat Chow is a registered trademark of Ralston Purina Company.

English type design by Susan Greenwood Schroeder.
Typeset in Gararond Bold.
Manufactured in Belgium.

Library of Congress Cataloging-in-Publication Data
 Schoch, Irène.
  [Hôtel d'été. English.]
  The cat's vacation / by Irène Schoch.
     p. cm.
 Summary: At your cat's invitation, Mr. and Mrs. Crocodile, the Penguin
family, and Mr. Moose sleep late, swim, and do all of the usual vacation
things at your house while you are away.
  ISBN 2-02-061884-2
  [1. Vacations—Fiction. 2. Cats—Fiction. 3. Animals—Fiction.]
  I. Title.
  PZ7.S36474Cat 2004
  [E]—dc22
  2003015016

Distributed in Canada by Raincoast Books
9050 Shaughnessy Street, Vancouver, British Columbia V6P 6E5

10 9 8 7 6 5 4 3 2 1

Chronicle Books LLC
85 Second Street, San Francisco, California 94105

www.chroniclekids.com

The Cat's Vacation

Irène Schoch

The Cat's Vacation

seuil chronicle

*H*ave you ever wondered what your cat does while you're on vacation?
When the nice lady from next door comes over to water the plants and
bring in the mail, she usually finds him taking a nap, just like any other
cat. But as soon as she leaves . . .

your cat has a vacation of his own.

"Ah! So glad you could make it! You're the first to arrive," says your cat to two huge crocodiles. "Come in and make yourself at home."

And taking their suitcases, he shows them into your parents' bedroom. After all, their bedroom is the nicest for grown-ups.

$\mathcal{T}$he crocodiles are very hungry after their long journey from the Nile
River in Egypt. So your cat cooks a big breakfast and brews a pot of coffee.

"Wonderful food!" says Mr. Crocodile.

"Better than Cat Chow," replies your cat.

Just then, the Penguin family arrives from the South Pole. Your cat shows
them into your bedroom. After all, it has the most toys—perfect for the
Penguin children.

$\mathcal{T}$he vacationers spend lazy afternoons relaxing in the backyard. Mr. Crocodile reads *A Thousand Miles Up the Nile*. The Penguin family cools down with ice-cream cones. Whenever they get thirsty, everyone helps themselves to the delicious cold lemonade made by your cat's best friend, Moose.

"What a nice break from playing with the same old toys and getting chased by the dog. Boy, I really needed a vacation!" says your cat, as he works on his tan.

One evening, when the guests come inside for dinner, they discover your cat's distant relatives have arrived after an exhausting trip from the jungles of India. Everyone is very careful not to disturb their nap, because they know that tigers can be very cranky.

But when the tigers wake up, they are very friendly and entertain everyone with music.

"Quick everybody, hide!" shouts your cat. It's your neighbor again—she doesn't seem to notice anything strange. Do you?

Before bedtime, everyone relaxes, and some of the guests play board games.

On rainy days, the only ones who can go outside to play are the penguins, because they don't need raincoats, of course. The other guests have to stay inside. But they don't mind, because your cat has made fresh apple pie. He is a very talented baker.

On the last night, the guests have a big party. Your cat puts on his chef's hat and fires up the grill. The party lasts all night long. Too bad you're not home to enjoy the fun!

Your cat's vacation has passed so quickly. It's already time for everyone to go. The guests from the Nile cry crocodile tears as they say good-bye.

"Careful not to forget anything! My family will be home very soon!" says your cat, hurrying everyone out the door.

As usual, Moose is the last to leave.

"You know what I hate about the end of the vacation?" says your cat.

"What?" asks Moose.

"Cleaning up!"

"I know what you mean," says Moose.

"Come on—we've got a lot to do!"

When you get home, your cat looks a little sad.

"Poor cat," you say, "you must have been so lonely without us . . ."

"Meow," your cat replies.

The End

(until next year)

Where did they all sleep?

① In your parents' bedroom: Mr. and Mrs. Crocodile

② In the office: the tigers

③ In your bedroom: the Penguin family

④ In the living room: Moose